For my parents – RB

BLOOMSBURY
CHILDREN'S
BOOKS

First published in Great Britain in 2000 by Bloomsbury Publishing Plc

38 Soho Square, London, W1D 3HB

This paperback edition first published 2001

The cover illustration for Who is It? and illustrations for pages 6-11 are published following consultation
with Cambridge University Press, publishers of Goldilocks and the Three Bears by Susan Price,
illustrated by Rosalind Beardshaw, published in Cambridge Reading by Cambridge University Press, 1999.

Text copyright © Sally Grindley 2000

Illustrations copyright © Rosalind Beardshaw 2000

The moral right of the author and illustrator has been asserted.

A CIP catalogue record for this book is available from the British Library.

ISBN 0 7475 5063 8 (Paperback)

ISBN 0 7475 4623 1 (Hardback)

Designed by Dawn Apperley

Printed by South China Printing Company

3 5 7 9 10 8 6 4 2

Who is it?

Sally Grindley and Rosalind Beardshaw

BLOOMSBURY
CHILDREN'S
BOOKS

Someone's eating
Mr Bear's porridge.

Someone's sitting in
Mrs Bear's chair.

Someone's sleeping
in Baby Bear's bed!

Who is it?

It's Goldilocks!

Wake up, Goldilocks.
The bears are
after you!

Someone's going into Grandma's cottage.

Someone's eating Grandma up.

Someone's wearing Grandma's night-clothes.

Who is it?

It's the Wolf!
Look out Little Red Riding Hood!

Someone's built a wooden
house under a bridge.

Someone hears
a trip-trapping
over his head.

Someone's feeling hungry
and he's ready to pounce!

Who is it?

It's the Troll!

Run away, Billy Goats Gruff!

Someone's climbing up
a great big beanstalk.

Someone's going
through a great big door.

Someone's stealing an enormous bag of gold!

Who is it?

It's Jack.
And the Giant's woken up!
Get out of there fast, Jack!

Someone's watching you
reading this book.

Someone can't wait till you
reach the last page.

Someone's ready with a **BIG** surprise for you.

Who is it?

It's me!

Acclaim for this book

'A marvellous new interpretation of favourite nursery tales ... a great book to share' PRACTICAL PRE-SCHOOL